people – cleverer than the detectives, cleverer than the people that they plan to rob or murder. But the criminals in these five stories are not always successful, and they meet some very surprising difficulties.

Sonia's boring little husband is only interested in his books and old silver. He has no idea what his wife and her lover plan to do – or does he? . . . A burglar whispering secrets on a train – how could he know that a thirteen-year-old girl can read his lips from the other side of the carriage? . . . Dunstan Thwaite decides he must do something about the man who is blackmailing him – it will look like an accident, of course . . . And Flambeau, the most famous thief in Europe, thinks it will be so easy to steal the Blue Cross from Father Brown, who is only a simple little priest . . . But perhaps it is safer not to do the crime yourself. If, like Mr Elliston, you pay another man to do the murder, nothing can possibly go wrong . . .

OXFORD BOOKWORMS LIBRARY
Crime & Mystery

As the Inspector Said
and Other Stories
Stage 3 (1000 headwords)

Series Editor: Jennifer Bassett
Founder Editor: Tricia Hedge
Activities Editors: Jennifer Bassett and Alison Baxter

RETOLD BY JOHN ESCOTT

As the Inspector Said
and Other Stories

OXFORD UNIVERSITY PRESS

OXFORD

UNIVERSITY PRESS

Great Clarendon Street, Oxford OX2 6DP

Oxford University Press is a department of the University of Oxford.
It furthers the University's objective of excellence in research, scholarship,
and education by publishing worldwide in

Oxford New York

Auckland Cape Town Dar es Salaam Hong Kong Karachi
Kuala Lumpur Madrid Melbourne Mexico City Nairobi
New Delhi Shanghai Taipei Toronto

With offices in

Argentina Austria Brazil Chile Czech Republic France Greece
Guatemala Hungary Italy Japan Poland Portugal Singapore
South Korea Switzerland Thailand Turkey Ukraine Vietnam

OXFORD and OXFORD ENGLISH are registered trade marks of
Oxford University Press in the UK and in certain other countries

ISBN 978 0 19 479108 3

A complete recording of this Bookworms edition of
As the Inspector Said and Other Stories is available on audio CD ISBN 978 0 19 479091 8

Printed in China

ACKNOWLEDGEMENTS

Illustrated by: Fiona MacVicar

*The publishers are grateful to the following
for their kind permission to adapt copyright material:*
A. P. Watt Ltd (on behalf of A. A. Gordon Clark) for *As the Inspector Said*
taken from *Best Detective Stories* by Cyril Hare; A. P. Watt Ltd (on behalf of
The Authors' Contingency Fund) for *The Railway Crossing*, which was
originally published as *The Level Crossing*; A. P. Watt Ltd (on
behalf of Jean Bell) for *Cash on Delivery*

Word count (main text): 9600 words

For more information on the Oxford Bookworms Library,
visit www.oup.com/bookworms

CONTENTS

INTRODUCTION   i

As the Inspector Said . . .   1
Cyril Hare

The Man Who Cut Off My Hair   6
Richard Marsh

The Railway Crossing   21
Freeman Wills Crofts

The Blue Cross   34
G. K. Chesterton

Cash on Delivery   49
Edmund Crispin

GLOSSARY   53
ACTIVITIES: Before Reading   58
ACTIVITIES: While Reading   60
ACTIVITIES: After Reading   62
ABOUT THE AUTHOR   67
ABOUT THE BOOKWORMS LIBRARY   69

AS THE INSPECTOR SAID ...
Cyril Hare

It is impossible to say when Charles Darrell and Sonia French first decided to murder Sonia's husband, Robert. Robert was nearly twice as old as Sonia, and he married her ten years before Charles Darrell came into her life. For eight of those years, Sonia was bored with her husband, although he did not seem to realize this. He was more interested in his books, and the silver which he bought.

Sonia and Charles were lovers for six months before things became difficult. People were beginning to talk, and it could not be long before Robert found out about them. 'Robert will never give me a divorce,' thought Sonia. 'And Charles and I have no money of our own.' But Sonia knew that Robert's silver alone was worth enough money to make life very comfortable for her and Charles.

By a strange accident, it was a policeman who gave them the idea for their murder plan. The inspector made a surprise visit to the Frenches' house one evening. Charles was also there. He often came in for a drink.

'There have been several burglaries near here,' the inspector told Robert, 'and we haven't caught the burglar. We know who he is, and it can't be long before we catch him, but we're very worried. He carries a gun, and we're almost sure he has killed a man. Now this house is in a very lonely place. Mr Darrell is your only neighbour. You also have a lot of valuable silver.'

'What are you trying to say?' asked Robert.

'I'm saying that it's sensible to be careful,' said the inspector. 'Very careful. Why not put your silver in the bank, until the burglar is caught?'

'I don't want to do that,' said Robert.

The inspector tried not to sound angry. 'Well, I have warned you, sir,' he said. 'Please remember that.'

The inspector left, and Charles said, 'The inspector didn't warn *me*. He knows *I've* nothing worth stealing. But if this gunman does visit me, he'll be sorry. I have a gun, and I won't think twice before using it.'

He was tall and strong, and Sonia thought he was very good-looking. And she did not try to hide her feelings.

'I feel sorry for the burglar who tries to frighten you, Charles,' she said.

Three nights later, Sonia was lying awake in her bed. Robert was asleep. It was ten minutes to two.

Sonia was excited. 'Ten minutes before Charles enters the house,' she thought. It was ten long minutes.

And then she heard a noise. Glass breaking, followed by the sound of a window as it was pushed up.

Robert did not wake up. Sonia waited until she heard the sound of Charles climbing through the open window, then she reached across to Robert's bed.

'Robert!' She was shaking him. 'Wake up. There's somebody downstairs!'

Robert woke slowly. 'What? Someone downstairs? No,

'It's sensible to be careful.'

I'm sure you're—' He sat up in bed, awake now. 'There *is* someone! I'll have to go down, I suppose.'

He put on his old grey dressing-gown, and went out of the room. Sonia waited in the dark. It seemed a very long wait, but it was less than half a minute. Then a thin line of light appeared under the bedroom door. Sonia heard her husband give a sudden cry, then she heard a gun explode. Something – or someone – heavy fell to the floor, then a door was banged open, and there was the sound of running feet outside the house.

3

Sonia waited. 'Charles must have time to escape before I call the police,' she thought.

She put on her bedside light and got out of bed. Now it was all over, she felt strangely calm. She knew what she was going to say to the police. How soon could she marry Charles? Six months from now? They could go to Venice for a holiday, after they were married. She had always wanted to see Venice . . .

Then the door opened.

And Robert walked in.

For a long moment, Sonia could only look at him, her stomach sick with fear. He looked back at her, silent, white-faced and untidy. But alive.

'What – what happened?' she said.

'He got away,' said Robert. 'I'm afraid he's taken some of my best silver with him. I wish now I had listened to the inspector and sent it to the bank.'

'But I heard a gun,' said Sonia. 'I thought you – you're not hurt, Robert?'

'No, Sonia, I'm not hurt,' said Robert. 'But I have some bad news. It's Charles. I think the dear, brave man was watching the house, and followed the burglar in, to try and help us. He's at the bottom of the stairs. I'm afraid there is nothing that we can do for him.'

Sonia fell forwards, her eyes closing, and Robert caught her. He carried her to the bed, then went downstairs. When he reached the bottom, he had to step over the body. He did this calmly, stepping around the blood on the carpet. But when he walked into the room where he kept his silver, he wanted to cry. All of the best pieces were gone.

He closed the door and went into his study. But before he telephoned the police, he was careful to clean the small gun that was in his dressing-gown pocket. Then he locked it inside his desk. He had taken care of the one problem in his usually very tidy life, and he wanted to make sure he would have no more trouble.

As the inspector said, it was sensible to be careful.

He was careful to clean the small gun that was in his dressing-gown pocket.

THE MAN WHO CUT OFF MY HAIR
Richard Marsh

My name is Judith Lee and I am a teacher. I teach people who are deaf and dumb, and I teach them by lip-reading. When people say a word, they all move their lips the same way, so if you watch them carefully, you know what they are saying.

My father was one of the first people to teach lip-reading. My mother was deaf, but she could lip-read, so lip-reading has always been part of my life. And because I have always been able to do it, I was able to play a part in the adventure I am going tell you about . . .

I was thirteen years old when it happened. My mother and father were visiting another country, and I was staying in a small village, in a cottage which we owned. Mrs Dickson, our servant, was staying there with me.

I was returning home by train one day, after a visit to some friends. There were two people sitting opposite me, a man and a woman. The woman got out at a station not far from my home. Then a man got in and sat beside the one who was already there. They seemed to know each other.

They talked quietly for some minutes, and it was impossible to hear what they said. But I only had to look at their faces. I was reading a magazine and looked up to see the first man say something which surprised me.

'. . . Myrtle Cottage. It's got a large myrtle tree in the front garden.'

The other man said something in a low voice, but his face was turned away from me. The first man replied, and I read his lips again. 'His name is Colegate, and he uses it as a summer cottage. He's got some of the best old silver in England.'

The other man shook his head and turned so I could see his face. I saw him say: 'Old silver is no better than new. You can only melt it.'

The first man's face became red. 'Only melt it! Don't be stupid! I can sell old silver at good prices. And that silver in Myrtle Cottage must be worth more than a thousand pounds. There's a silver salt-cellar worth at least a hundred.'

The other man looked at me while I was watching his friend speak. He had fair hair and blue eyes. 'That child is watching us,' he whispered. 'Be careful.'

The look in those blue eyes began to frighten me.

The first man said, 'Let her watch, she can't hear us.'

I was alone with them, and I was quite small. So I looked back at my magazine instead of watching the rest of their conversation. I knew Myrtle Cottage because it was not very far from our own cottage. And I knew Mr Colegate, and about his old silver. I knew the silver salt-cellar the two men spoke about, and wondered why they were interested in it. I was very young. I did not think: 'These two men who speak in whispers may not be honest.'

They both got out at the station before our village.

After tea that evening, I went for a walk without telling Mrs Dickson. My walk took me past Myrtle Cottage. It was

'*That child is watching us.*'

ITEMS ON ISSUE
FOR Mr Padam Ale
ON 24/10/17 17:15:30

Goodbye, Mr Hollywood/Escott,
John.
91120000165370 DUE
14/11/17
Lady Chatterley ka
premi/Lawrence, R. H.
91100000112466 DUE
14/11/17
Oxford Bookworms Library:
Stage 3: As th
91120000163722 DUE
14/11/17

small, and there were no other houses near it. I knew that Mr Colegate was away, but when I went into the garden, I saw that the front-room window was open. I looked inside. What I saw surprised me very much.

In the room was the first man from the train. All of Mr Colegate's silver was on the table in front of him, and he was holding the silver salt-cellar. I did not know what to think. What was he doing there? What should I do? I was still trying to decide when a hand went round my throat.

'If you make a sound, I'll kill you,' said a man's voice in my ear. 'Believe me, I will!'

It was the other man, and he recognised me.

'It's the girl from the train!' he said.

The first man came to the window. 'What's happening?' he asked. 'Who's that child you're holding?'

The other man pushed my face forwards. 'Can't you see? I *knew* she was listening!'

'She couldn't hear us on the train,' said the first man. 'Nobody could hear our whispers. Give her to me.'

I was passed through the window, and now it was his hands that went round my throat. 'Who are you?' he wanted to know. 'If you scream, I'll pull your head right off you!'

I did not move or speak.

'Cut her throat,' said the other man, and took a long, terrible-looking knife with a silver handle from the table.

'Wait,' said his friend. He took a piece of rope from his bag. Then they pushed me into a chair and tied the rope around my arms and legs. They also tied something across my mouth to stop me speaking.

The man with blue eyes moved towards me with the knife. I was sure he was going to cut my throat. But he took my long hair in one hand, and with that terrible knife he cut all of it from my head!

I was more angry than I thought possible. I wanted to take that knife and push it into him! My long hair was more valuable to me than almost anything. Not because of my own love of it, but because my mother loved it. It pleased her so much, and she often told me how beautiful it was. And now this man had robbed me of it in the most terrible way. At that moment, I wanted to kill him.

He hit me across the face with my own hair. 'It didn't take me long to cut it off,' he said, 'but I'll cut your throat quicker if you try to move.'

The first man said, 'Leave her alone. She can't move and she can't make a sound. Come over here and help me.'

The man with blue eyes let my hair fall all over me. Then the two of them began to put Mr Colegate's silver into two large bags. That was when I realized they were stealing it, and there was nothing I could do.

The man with blue eyes moved towards the window, carrying one of the bags. The first man put a hand on his arm, and I watched him whisper, 'Do you remember the plan?'

The man with blue eyes put his mouth close to the other man's ear. I watched his lips as he said, 'Cotterill, Cloakroom, Victoria Station, Brighton Railway.'

I knew the words were important and promised myself

The man with blue eyes moved towards me with the knife.

that I would not forget them.

He got out of the window and his bag was passed to him. He turned towards me and said, 'Sorry I can't take a piece of your hair. Perhaps I'll come back for some later.' Then he went, and anger burned inside me.

His friend did not look at me. He took his bag and went out through the door. I don't know what happened to him afterwards. I was left alone, all through that night.

I was not afraid, but the rope hurt my arms and legs. I repeated the words, 'Cotterill, Cloakroom, Victoria Station, Brighton Railway.' I was sure they were important.

I did not sleep that night. Day came, and I wondered what Mrs Dickson was doing. Was she looking for me? I had some friends who lived three or four miles away. Sometimes I stayed the night with them, without telling anyone at home. Did Mrs Dickson think I was with them?

I do not know what time it was when I heard the sound of feet outside. The day seemed almost over. I watched the open window, and suddenly a face appeared.

It was Mr Colegate.

'Judith!' he said. 'Judith Lee!'

He was not a young man, but he climbed in through that window as quickly as a boy. He took a knife from his pocket and cut the rope around my arms and legs, then he uncovered my mouth and at last I could speak.

'Cotterill, Cloakroom, Victoria Station, Brighton Railway,' I said. Then I fell into Mr Colegate's arms.

✳ ✳ ✳

I knew no more until I woke up in bed with Mrs Dickson standing beside me. With her were Dr Scott, Mr Colegate, Pierce the village policeman, and another man. I discovered later that he was a detective.

I saw that I was in a room in Myrtle Cottage, and sat up in bed – and remembered everything.

'He cut off my hair with the long knife!' I said.

My head felt strange. I asked for a mirror, then became angry again when I saw the blue-eyed man's work. Before anyone could stop me, I jumped out of bed.

'Cotterill, Cloakroom, Victoria Station, Brighton Railway,' I said. 'Where are my clothes?'

At first they thought I was crazy. But then I told them my story. 'Cotterill, Cloakroom, Victoria Station, Brighton Railway,' I said again. 'That's where I'm going to catch the man who cut off my hair. And if we don't go quickly, we may be too late.'

Mr Colegate agreed. He wanted to get his silver back as much as I wanted to find the man who cut my hair. So we went up to London on the first train that we could catch – Mr Colegate, the detective, and an almost hairless child.

We got to Victoria Station and went to the cloakroom.

'Is there a parcel here in the name of Cotterill?' asked the detective.

'One in the name of Cotterill was taken only half a minute ago,' the cloakroom man replied. 'Didn't you see him walking off with it?' He looked along the station. 'There he is! Someone's going to speak to him.'

13

'*Cotterill, Cloakroom, Victoria Station, Brighton Railway.*'

I saw a man carrying a parcel, and I saw the man who was going to speak to him. 'It's the man who cut my hair!' I shouted, and ran towards him as fast as I could go. He looked round and saw me, and quickly realized who I was. He whispered to the man with the parcel before running away.

I saw clearly what he said. 'Bantock, 13 Harwood Street, near Oxford Street.' Those were the words. And then he turned and ran away. Mr Colegate and the detective were close behind me. The man with the parcel saw us, and at once he dropped the parcel and ran off.

We did not catch him, or the man who cut my hair. The station was full of people coming off a train, which made it easy for both men to escape. But we got the parcel. It was not big enough to contain Mr Colegate's silver, we realized that. But it *did* contain a much bigger surprise.

Jewels!

A London detective was sent for. He looked at the jewels and said, 'These are the Duchess of Dachet's jewels. The police all over Europe are looking for them.'

The man from the cloakroom was with us. 'That parcel has been with us for nearly a month,' he said. 'The person who took it out paid for twenty-seven days.'

'I wish I could catch him,' said the London detective. 'I have a word or two that I want to say to him.'

'I think I know where you can find him,' I said. 'Bantock, 13 Harwood Street, near Oxford Street.'

'Who is Bantock?' the detective asked.

Jewels!

'I don't know,' I said. 'But I saw the man who cut off my hair whisper those words before he ran away.'

'You saw him whisper them?' The London detective looked at the others. 'What does she mean? Young lady, you were fifteen metres away. How could you hear him whisper?'

'I didn't say I heard him whisper,' I replied. 'I said I *saw* him. I don't need to hear to know what a person is saying.'

'Judith is an excellent lip-reader,' said Mr Colegate. He explained, but the others found it hard to believe.

'So what did you see him whisper?' asked the detective.

'I'll tell you if I can come with you,' I said.

The detective laughed. He seemed to think that I was amusing, but I don't know why. He did not understand how angry I was about my hair. 'All right,' he said. 'You can come. Now, tell me what you saw him whisper.'

So I told him again and he wrote it down.

'I know Harwood Street, but I don't know Mr Bantock,' he said. 'First I'll send a message for some help, then we'll go and visit Mr Bantock – if there *is* a Mr Bantock.'

The four of us went in a taxi – the two detectives, Mr Colegate and I. After a while, the taxi stopped on the corner of a street.

'This is Harwood Street,' said the London detective. 'We can walk the rest of the way. We don't want a taxi to stop outside the door. They may guess who we are.'

It was a street full of shops. The shop at number 13 sold jewels and other less valuable things. The name 'Bantock' was over the top of the window.

As we reached the shop, a taxi stopped outside it and five men got out. The London detective recognized them and did not look pleased. 'Now our visit won't be a surprise,' he said. 'Come on, let's go in quickly.'

And we went in, the detective first and me behind him. There were two young men standing close together at the other side of the shop. When they saw us, I saw one whisper, 'They're detectives! Ring the alarm bell!'

'He's going to ring the alarm bell!' I shouted.

The men from the other taxi were also detectives.

They came in quickly and held each of the two young men.

There was a door at the end of the shop which the London detective opened. 'Stairs,' he said. 'We'll go up. You men wait here until you're wanted.'

I followed him up the stairs. At the top were two more doors. I could hear voices coming from behind one of them. The London detective went towards it. He opened the door and went in, and I was close behind him. There were several men in there, but I was only interested in one. He was standing on the other side of a table.

'That's the man who cut off my hair!' I cried.

He seemed at first like a man who had seen a ghost, but then he said, 'I wish I had cut your throat!'

The police caught all the thieves. They were wanted all over the world for other robberies. Mr Colegate got his silver back. Mr Bantock, who owned the shop, was someone who bought and sold stolen jewels. He and all the other men in

'That's the man who cut off my hair.'

that room were sent to prison.

It took many years for my hair to grow long again, and it never grew as long as before. Each time I looked into a mirror, some of my anger returned.

But the man who cut my hair was stupid. *Before* he cut it, the rope hurt me badly and I wasn't interested in what he and his friend were doing or saying. But *after* he cut it, I was very angry indeed, and so I watched every move which they – *and their lips!* – made!

THE RAILWAY CROSSING
Freeman Wills Crofts

Dunstan Thwaite looked at the railway crossing and decided that it was time for John Dunn to die. It was a very suitable place for a murder. There were trees all around, and they hid the trains which came so fast along the railway line. The nearest house was Thwaite's own, and this was also hidden by the trees. People and traffic did not use the crossing very often, and the big gates were kept locked. There was a small gate used by passengers going to the station, but at night it was always quiet.

Thwaite was a worried man. He had to use sleeping powders to help him sleep. But after tonight, things were going to be different. The time had come to stop the blackmail. The time had come for John Dunn to die.

It all began five years earlier . . .

Thwaite worked in the offices of a large company, and his only money was the money that the company paid him. It was not much, but it was enough. Then he met the beautiful Miss Hilda Lorraine and asked her to marry him.

She came from an important family who were supposed to be very rich, but in fact they had less money than Thwaite had thought. He learned that he would have to pay for the wedding himself. And he did not have enough money for the expensive kind of wedding that Miss Lorraine wanted. So Thwaite stole a thousand pounds, by changing the figures in the company's books. He planned to put the money back after he was married, but someone discovered that it was missing.

Thwaite kept quiet. Another man was thought to be the thief, and he lost his job. Thwaite still said nothing.

But John Dunn worked in the same office. He worked closely with Thwaite and guessed Thwaite's crime. He searched through the company's books until he found what he was looking for. Then he went to Thwaite.

'Sorry to have to ask you, Mr Thwaite,' he said. 'I need a hundred pounds . . . for my son. He's in a bit of trouble, you see . . .'

'But you don't have a son,' said Thwaite.

Dunn just smiled. It wasn't a very nice smile. 'A hundred pounds,' he said again.

And then Thwaite knew that he was being blackmailed.

He paid Dunn one hundred pounds, and Dunn said nothing more for a year. During that time, Thwaite got married.

Then the day came when Dunn asked him for more money.

'Two hundred and fifty pounds,' he said to Thwaite.

'I can't pay—' began Thwaite.

But he did. Either he paid or he went to prison.

It went on for five years, and each time Dunn wanted more money. Thwaite found it difficult to live on the money that he was left with. His wife liked expensive things. An expensive house, an expensive car, visits to expensive

'*A hundred pounds,*' *he said again.*

restaurants. She also discovered that some of the money her husband was paid each year seemed to disappear. He tried to lie about it, but he knew that she thought he was paying to keep another woman.

Oh, how he hated John Dunn! Something must happen!

And then he remembered the railway crossing.

It was not a new idea. Weeks before, he had thought about what *could* happen there. The idea came when the doctor gave him some powders to help him sleep. He thought about giving Dunn enough of them to kill him, but then he got a better idea. Although he was afraid, Thwaite slowly realized that murder was the only answer to his problem.

Then Dunn asked for more money.

'Five hundred pounds, Mr Thwaite,' Dunn told him.

'Five hundred!' said Thwaite. 'Why not ask for the moon? You'll get neither one nor the other.'

'Five hundred,' repeated Dunn, calmly.

It was then that Thwaite decided to murder the other man. He pretended to think about the money for a moment, then he said, 'Come to my house tomorrow night and we'll talk.' He remembered his wife was going to be away in London all night. 'And bring those papers from the office which you want me to look at.'

'All right,' said Dunn.

The following evening, Thwaite put two hundred pounds in his pocket. Then he put half of one of his sleeping powders into a whisky bottle. There was only enough whisky for two glasses, but there was an unopened bottle next to it. Next he put a hammer into one pocket of his overcoat, and a torch into the other pocket. The coat was outside the door of his study. Lastly, he moved the hands on his watch and on the study clock forward by ten minutes. Those extra ten minutes would give him his alibi.

Thwaite knew that he must be extra careful. He knew that people at the office thought there was some secret between him and Dunn. A secret that Thwaite didn't want anyone to know.

'If Dunn is killed,' he thought, 'they'll wonder if it was really an accident, or if I murdered him.'

But if his plan went well, the police would believe that he hadn't left the house.

Thwaite sat down to wait for John Dunn. He thought about what he was going to do. Murder! He could almost see his hand holding the hammer above Dunn; could hear the awful sound of it crashing down on to the man's head. He could see Dunn's dead body! Dead all except the eyes, which looked at Thwaite . . . followed him everywhere he went . . .

He tried to calm himself. He remembered why he was doing this. When Dunn was dead, his problems were over.

Half an hour later, Dunn arrived. Jane opened the door. Jane was the servant who lived in the house with Thwaite and his wife. She brought Dunn into the study.

Thwaite smiled in a friendly way. 'Oh, good. You've brought those papers for me to see, Dunn. Thank you.'

After Jane left, the two men looked at each other.

'Give me the papers,' Thwaite said. 'I'll look at them now

*Next he put a hammer into one pocket of his overcoat,
and a torch into the other pocket.*

that you've brought them.' Fifteen minutes later, he gave the papers back to Dunn and sat back in his chair. 'Now, about that other matter.' He got up. 'But why not have a drink first?'

'No, thank you,' said Dunn. He looked afraid.

'What are you afraid of?' said Thwaite. He gave Dunn the opened whisky bottle and two glasses. 'We can both drink the same whisky, if you like. Here, you do it.'

After a moment, Dunn put whisky into each glass, then he waited until Thwaite drank before he drank his own. Thwaite watched him. How long before the other man began to feel sleepy? Thwaite needed all of one sleeping powder to make *him* sleep, but Dunn did not usually take them.

'Listen, Dunn,' said Thwaite, 'I haven't got five hundred pounds, but I can give you this.' He took the money from his pocket and put it on the table.

Dunn counted it. 'Two hundred?' he said, with a laugh. 'Are you trying to be funny?'

'I'm not saying it will be the last,' said Thwaite. 'Take it now and be pleased that you've got it.'

Dunn shook his head. 'Five hundred, Mr Thwaite.'

'I've told you, I can't do it,' said Thwaite. 'And I won't do it. You can tell everyone what I did – I don't care any more. It's been five years, and I've done a lot of good work for the company during that time. I saved them a lot more than a thousand pounds. I'll sell this house and pay them back. I'll take my punishment, then I'll go and live in another country and give myself a new name.'

'And your wife?' said Dunn.

'My wife will leave the country first,' Thwaite told him. 'She'll wait for me to come out of prison. It won't be more than two or three years. So you can take the two hundred pounds, or you can do your worst!'

The powder in the whisky was beginning to make Dunn sleepy. He looked stupidly at Thwaite, and Thwaite began to worry. Had he given the other man too much? He looked at the clock. There was not much time left.

'Will you take it, or leave it?' asked Thwaite.

'Five hundred,' said Dunn, in a heavy voice. 'I want five hundred.'

'You can go and do your worst,' said Thwaite.

Dunn held out a shaking hand. 'Come on, pay me.'

Thwaite began to worry again. 'Are you feeling all right, Dunn? Have some more whisky.' He opened the other bottle and put some whisky in Dunn's glass. Dunn drank it, and it seemed to make him feel better.

'That was strange,' he said. 'I didn't feel very well, but I feel a little better now.'

'If you're going to catch your train, you must go,' said Thwaite. 'Tell me tomorrow what you finally decide to do. Take the two hundred with you.'

Dunn thought for a moment, then picked up the money. He looked at his watch, then looked at the study clock. 'Your clock is wrong,' he said. 'I have ten more minutes.'

'Wrong?' said Thwaite. He looked at his own watch. 'It's your watch that's wrong. Look at mine.'

Dunn looked and seemed unable to understand it. He

stood up . . . and almost fell back again.

Thwaite hid a smile. This was how he wanted Dunn to be. 'You're not feeling well,' he said. 'I'll take you to the station. Wait until I get my coat.'

Now that the time was here, Thwaite felt cool and calm. He put on his coat, feeling the hammer in the pocket, then went back into the study.

'We'll go out this way,' he said.

There was a side door from the study into the garden. Thwaite closed it silently and it locked automatically behind him. It was his plan to return that way, go in quietly again, and then to change the clock and his watch back to the right time. Then he would shout 'Goodnight', and close the front door very loudly, pretending that somebody had left just then. Next, he would call Jane and ask for some coffee, making sure that she saw the clock. Then, if the police asked her later, Jane could say that Thwaite did not leave the house and that Dunn went to catch his train at the right time.

It was a dry night, but very dark. A train carrying freight went slowly by. Thwaite smiled to himself. There were plenty of freight trains at that time of the night. He needed one of them to hide his crime for him. He planned to hit Dunn on the head with the hammer, then put his body on the railway line. A freight train would do the rest.

Slowly, the two men walked on, Thwaite holding Dunn's arm. A light wind moved among the trees. Thwaite gently pushed the half-asleep Dunn forwards. He put his hand into his pocket for the hammer . . .

And stopped.

His keys! They were still inside the house, and he could not get back in without them! He would have to ring the front door bell. His alibi was destroyed!

It was a bad mistake. Everything was wrong now. He couldn't go on with the murder.

'Most murderers make mistakes,' thought Thwaite, trying to calm himself. 'I've been the same.' But he was shaking with fear as he thought about the mistake. Suddenly, he could not walk another step with Dunn.

'Goodnight,' he said to the other man.

And before they reached the crossing, he turned and walked back to the house.

For ten minutes, Thwaite walked up and down outside until he began to feel calm again. Then he rang the bell.

A few moments later, Jane opened the door.

'Thank you, Jane,' he said. 'I went to see Mr Dunn over the crossing, and I forgot my keys.'

He went to bed a happier man. He was not a murderer.

When he was eating his breakfast the next morning, he decided what to do. 'I'll tell them at the office that I stole the thousand pounds,' he said to himself. 'I'll take my punishment, and then I can have some peace again.'

It suddenly seemed so easy.

Until Jane came in.

'Have you heard the news, sir?' she said. 'Mr Dunn was killed by a train on the crossing last night. A man who was working on the railway line found him this morning.'

His keys! They were still inside the house.

Thwaite slowly went white. Jane was looking at him strangely. What was she thinking? What story did he tell her the night before? He couldn't remember!

'Dunn killed!' he said. 'How terrible, Jane! I'll go down.'

The body was in a small railway building, near the line. There was a policeman outside.

'A sad accident, Mr Thwaite,' the policeman said. 'You knew the man, didn't you, sir?'

'He worked in my office,' replied Thwaite. 'He was with me last night, discussing business. I suppose this happened on his way home. It's terrible!'

'It's very sad, sir,' said the policeman. 'But accidents will happen.'

'I know that,' said Thwaite. 'But I wish he hadn't drunk so much of my whisky. I was going to walk with him to the station.'

The policeman looked closely at Thwaite. 'And did you, sir?'

'No,' said Thwaite. 'The cold night air seemed to make him feel better. I turned back before the crossing.'

The policeman said no more, but later that day two more policemen came to the office. 'Have they talked to Jane?' wondered Thwaite. Again he told them, 'I left Dunn before we reached the railway crossing.' They wrote down what he said to them, then went away.

Next day, they came back.

There were things that Thwaite could not explain to them. Why did the whisky bottle contain what was left of a sleeping powder? Why was the study clock wrong by ten minutes? (At dinner-time earlier on the same evening, Jane had noticed that it was right.) And why was a hammer found in his overcoat pocket?

Then the police found papers in Dunn's house. The handwriting on them was Dunn's. It told the story of Thwaite and the thousand pounds, and it told how Thwaite was a thief. The police then discovered that money taken from Thwaite's bank account over the last five years always appeared a few days later in Dunn's bank book.

Lastly, the time of death was known to be 10.30 pm because Dunn's blood was found on the train that went through the railway crossing at that time. *It was also seven minutes before Jane opened the front door to let Thwaite back in.*

At first, Thwaite had no answers to all their questions.

Finally, on his last morning, he told them the true story. Then he went to his death bravely.

THE BLUE CROSS
G.K. *Chesterton*

The man who got off the boat at Harwich had a short black beard. There was nothing to show that he had a gun in his coat pocket, and nothing to show that he was one of the cleverest men in Europe. He was Valentin, the chief of the Paris police, and the most famous detective in the world. He was coming from Brussels to London to make the most important arrest of the century. Flambeau was in England, and the police of three countries were trying to catch this famous thief.

In London there was a big meeting of priests from all over the world, and Valentin was guessing that Flambeau would use this meeting for some criminal plan or other. Flambeau was strong and clever, and he enjoyed a joke.

Once, he ran down the Rue de Rivoli with a policeman under one arm.

But how was Valentin to find Flambeau? There was one thing to help him. Flambeau could put on other clothes, or change the way he looked, but he was a very tall man and could not hide it. Because of this, Valentin was sure that Flambeau was not on the boat.

He was also sure that Flambeau did not get on the train going from Harwich to London. Only six other people got on during the journey. One short railwayman, three short farmers, one very short woman, and a very short priest going up to London from an Essex village.

When Valentin saw this last person, he almost laughed. The little priest had a round, simple face. He had several parcels which he found difficult to keep together, and a large umbrella which often fell to the floor. Many priests would be coming to London that day, Valentin thought. Coming from their quiet little towns and villages. This one was explaining to everyone that he must be careful because he was carrying something made of real silver 'with blue stones' in one of the parcels.

He got off the train at Stratford in east London with all his parcels, and came back for his umbrella. When he did, Valentin warned him not to tell everyone about his silver 'with blue stones'.

The detective was looking for people who were at least two metres tall, because Flambeau was several centimetres taller than this. He got off the train in central London and went to the London police to ask for help if he needed it. Then he went for a long walk.

He stopped suddenly in a quiet square. On one side the buildings were higher than the rest, and there was a small restaurant between the tall houses. It stood high above the street, with steps going up to the front door. Valentin stood looking at it, smoking a cigarette. When he was looking for a criminal, if he had a clue, he followed it. If he had no clue at all, he followed his own feelings. A man must begin somewhere. And something about the quiet little restaurant made Valentin want to start there. He went up the steps, sat down by the window, and asked for a cup of coffee.

The little priest had a round, simple face.

A few minutes later, Valentin was lifting the cup to his lips. But he put it down quickly. 'I've put salt in it,' he said, and he looked at the bowl of silvery powder. It was a sugar bowl. So why did they keep salt in it? There were two full salt-cellars on his table. What was in them? He tasted it. It was sugar.

He looked around. Except for one or two dark wet stains on the white wall, there was nothing at all strange in that place. Valentin called the waiter and asked him to taste the sugar. The waiter was half-asleep, but he woke up when he tasted the sugar.

'Do you play this joke on your customers every morning?' asked Valentin.

The waiter did not know what to say. Then, suddenly, he said, 'It was the two priests.'

'What two priests?' said Valentin.

'The two priests who threw soup at the wall over there,' replied the waiter.

Valentin looked again at the dark wet stains.

'The two of them came in and drank soup here very early this morning,' the waiter explained. 'They were both very quiet. One of them paid the bill and went out. The other took several more minutes to get his things together. Then he picked up his cup, which was only half empty, and threw it at the wall. I was in the back room, but I ran out to find the restaurant empty. I tried to catch them in the street, but they were too far away. They went round the corner into Carstairs Street.'

The detective jumped to his feet, put on his hat, and paid

his bill. A moment later, he was outside.

He walked round into the next street. Although he was excited and in a hurry, Valentin saw something in the front of a shop that made him stop. The shop sold fruit, and there were some oranges and some nuts at the front. They each had cards with writing on them. The card on the nuts said: 'Best oranges, two for a penny.' The card on the oranges said: 'Best nuts, four pence for a bag.'

Valentin looked at the two cards. 'I've seen this kind of joke before,' he thought.

He told the man in the shop about the cards. The man said nothing, but he put the cards in the right places.

'Can I ask you a question?' said Valentin. 'If two cards in a shop are in the wrong places, how are they like a priest's hat that has come to London for a holiday? Or, why do nuts that are said to be oranges make me think of two priests, one tall and the other short?'

The man in the shop looked angry. 'Are you a friend of theirs?' he said. 'If you are, you can tell them that I'll bang their stupid heads together if they knock over my apples again!'

'Did they knock over your apples?' asked the detective.

'One of them did,' said the man.

'Which way did they go?' asked Valentin.

'Up that second road on the left-hand side, and then across the square,' answered the man.

'Thanks,' said Valentin, and hurried away. On the other side of the second square, he found a policeman. 'Have you seen two priests?' he asked.

The policeman laughed. 'I have, sir. One of them stood in the middle of the road, dropping parcels everywhere.'

'Which way did they go?' asked Valentin.

'They went on one of those yellow buses over there,' answered the policeman. 'Those that go to Hampstead.'

Valentin told the policeman who he was, then said, 'Call two of your men to come with me.'

In two minutes, an inspector and another detective arrived. 'Well, sir,' began the inspector. 'How—?'

'I'll tell you on the top of that bus,' said Valentin.

When the three of them were sitting on the top seats, the inspector said, 'A taxi is quicker.'

'True,' said Valentin. 'But we don't know where we're going. All we can do is look for some strange thing.'

'What kind of strange thing?' asked the inspector.

'Any kind of strange thing,' replied Valentin.

The yellow bus went slowly up the roads to the north of the city. The French detective became quiet. Lunch-time came and went, and the long roads seemed to go on for ever. Valentin sat silently and watched everything that went by.

The two other detectives were almost asleep when he suddenly shouted. They quickly followed Valentin off the bus without knowing why.

'Over there!' said Valentin. 'The place with the broken window!' He was looking at a restaurant. It had a large window with a hole in the middle of the glass.

'How do we know that the window has anything to do with them?' asked the inspector.

'The place with the broken window!'

Valentin became angry. '*Know?*' he said. 'We can't *know*. But don't you understand? We must either follow one wild chance, or go home to bed.'

They followed him into the restaurant where the three of them ate a meal at a small table. Valentin looked at the little star of broken glass, but learned nothing from it.

'Your window is broken,' he said, paying his bill.

'Yes, sir,' replied the waiter. 'It was very strange how it happened.'

'Tell me,' said Valentin.

'Two of those priests came in,' said the waiter. 'Those foreign priests who are in the city at the moment. They had a cheap and quiet little lunch, and one of them paid for it and went out. The other was just going to follow him when I realized something. "Wait!" I said to the one who was nearly out of the door. "You've paid too much." And I picked up the bill to show him. But I got a surprise.'

'What do you mean?' asked Valentin.

'I was sure that I'd put four shillings on that bill,' said the waiter. 'But now I saw that it was fourteen.'

'Then what happened?' said Valentin.

'The priest at the door said, "That will pay for the window." "What window?" I asked. "The one that I'm going to break," he said. And he broke the window with his umbrella! I went after him, but I wasn't quick enough. They went up Bullock Street so fast, I couldn't catch them.'

'Bullock Street!' said Valentin, and he ran up that road as quickly as the strange pair that he was following.

Their journey took them through dark, narrow streets, and the inspector guessed that they would finally reach some part of Hampstead Heath. Suddenly, Valentin stopped in front of a small, brightly-lit sweet-shop. After a moment, he went inside and bought some chocolate. He began to ask the shop woman a question, but she spoke first.

She saw the inspector behind him and immediately said, 'If you're the police and you've come about that parcel, I've already sent it off.'

'Parcel!' repeated Valentin.

'I mean the parcel that the priest left,' said the woman.

'Quickly!' said Valentin. 'Tell us what happened!'

'They came in half an hour ago,' said the woman. 'They bought some sweets, and then went off towards the Heath. Then one ran back into the shop and said, "Did I leave a parcel?" I looked around but couldn't see one. He said, "Never mind. But if you do find it, please send it to this address." He left the address, and a shilling for me. But after he went, I looked again and found that there *was* a parcel, so I posted it. I can't remember the address now, but it was somewhere in Westminster.'

'Is Hampstead Heath near here?' asked Valentin.

'Straight on for fifteen minutes,' said the woman.

Valentin hurried out and began to run. The others followed him. The street they went through was full of evening shadows. Then they were out on the open Heath, and Valentin saw the two black shapes that he was looking for.

They were a long way away, but Valentin saw that one

'If you're the police and you've come about that parcel,
I've already sent it off.'

was smaller than the other, and that the bigger man was over two metres tall. He hurried on. As he got closer, he saw something surprising, but something which he had already guessed. The small man was the priest from the Harwich train, the one who had talked about his parcels.

Earlier that day, Valentin had discovered that a Father Brown from Essex was bringing a very old silver cross, with valuable blue jewels, to show to some of the foreign priests who were meeting in London. Valentin was sure that if *he* was able to find out about this, then Flambeau was able to find out, too. He was also sure that Flambeau planned to steal the cross. And it was not surprising that Flambeau, looking and talking like a priest, had been able to make the simple little man come to Hampstead Heath. What Valentin could not understand were the strange clues that had brought him there too. Soup on a wall, nuts called oranges, and broken windows.

The detectives followed the two across the wilder part of the Heath, then lost them for a few minutes. When they saw them again, the two priests were sitting on a seat, having a serious conversation. Valentin and his friends hid behind a tree and listened to them talking.

It was then that Valentin began to wonder if he was right. The two men on the seat were talking calmly about the ideas of their church. Valentin could almost hear the other two detectives laughing at him. They had come all this way, only to listen to the talk of two gentle old priests!

Father Brown was speaking. 'Look at the stars, like jewels in the sky. But even in those other worlds, there must be some laws of reason and goodness.' Valentin was about to move away, but the words of the tall priest stopped him.

'Who can understand the mystery of the stars?' Then he added calmly, 'Just give me the silver cross, will you? We're all alone here, and I could pull you to pieces easily.'

The small priest did not move. He continued to look up at the stars. Perhaps he had not understood. Or perhaps he was too afraid to move.

'Yes,' said the tall priest, in the same low voice. 'I am Flambeau. Now, give me that cross.'

'No,' replied the other priest.

'*Just give me the silver cross, will you?*'

Flambeau suddenly laughed. 'No, you won't give it to me, you simple little priest,' he said, 'because I already have it in my pocket!'

The small man looked at him. 'Are you sure?'

Flambeau laughed again. 'Yes, you stupid man. I knew which of your parcels contained the jewelled cross, so I made a careful copy of the parcel. And now you, my friend, have that copy parcel and I have the jewels. It's easily done, Father Brown, easily done!'

Father Brown did not look worried. 'Yes, very easily. I remember another man who used copy parcels for many years,' he said. 'I remembered him when I began to wonder about you.'

'Wonder about me?' said Flambeau. 'When did you begin to wonder about me? When I brought you up to the Heath?'

'No, no,' said Father Brown. 'When we first met. I saw that little shape under the arm of your coat, where you keep your knife.'

'How did you know that?' cried Flambeau.

'When I was a priest in Hartlepool,' said Father Brown, 'there were three men who hid their knives in the same way. So I watched you. I saw you change the parcels . . . and I changed them back. Then I left the right one behind.'

'Left it behind?' repeated Flambeau.

'I went back to the sweet-shop,' explained Father Brown, 'and asked the woman if she saw me leave a parcel. Then I gave her an address if it was found. I knew I hadn't left a parcel, but when I went away again, I did leave one. She has posted it to a friend of mine in Westminster.' He went on sadly, 'I learnt that from a man in Hartlepool, too. He did it with handbags which he stole at railway stations, but he's a good man now. People tell priests things, you see.'

Flambeau pulled a parcel from his pocket and opened it. There was only paper and stones inside it. He jumped up angrily and shouted, 'I don't believe you. You've got the silver cross on you, and I'm going to take it from you!'

'No,' said Father Brown, and he stood up. 'You won't take it from me. First, because I really haven't got it. And second, because we are not alone. Behind that tree are two strong policemen and the cleverest detective alive. How did they come here? I'll tell you. I wasn't sure if you were a thief, so I tried several things. A man usually says if he finds salt in his coffee. If he doesn't, he has a reason for keeping quiet. I changed the salt and sugar, and *you* kept quiet. A man usually says if his bill is too big. If he doesn't, he has a reason for saying nothing. I changed your bill, and *you* paid it.'

Flambeau did not seem to be able to move.

'I wanted to be sure the police could follow us,' Father Brown went on. 'At every place we went to, I did something which people would talk about. Only little things – a soup stain on a wall, some apples that were knocked over, a broken window. But I saved the cross.'

'How do you know all these things?' cried Flambeau.

The shadow of a smile went across the round face of Father Brown. 'By being a simple little priest, I suppose,' he said. 'If you listen to enough men telling you about their crimes, you are sure to learn something.'

The three policemen moved out from behind the tree.

Flambeau knew when he had lost a battle, and he was famous for his politeness. He took off his hat to Valentin and smiled.

'Do not take your hat off to me, my friend,' said Valentin. 'Let us both take them off to Father Brown.'

And they both stood with their hats off while the little Essex priest looked around for his umbrella.

And they both stood with their hats off while the little Essex priest looked around for his umbrella.

CASH ON DELIVERY
Edmund Crispin

Max Linster went through the small side gate and saw the large house in front of him. Not far away, a church clock told him that it was ten o'clock. He had half an hour to do the job. At midnight, a private plane would take off for Europe from a lonely field in Norfolk, and Linster planned to be on it even if his last job in England was not successful.

He walked towards the house and saw a room with a light on. He looked quickly through the window and saw that it was the servants' room. Then he moved round the building and climbed to the upstairs room that his orders had described. It was not difficult to reach, and the window was unlocked, as promised.

He stepped inside, and waited.

After a moment, he heard someone coming and moved quickly and silently across to the door. He hid behind it. It opened slowly. Someone put on the light. The man who came in was about thirty-five years old. He had fair hair, and the right arm of his coat was empty.

'Mr Elliston?' Linster said from behind him.

Jacob Elliston turned quickly. He looked at Linster for a moment, then said, 'So you're the person they sent.'

'I'm who they sent,' agreed Linster.

Elliston closed the door. 'We have to be quick,' he said. 'You have guessed that this is my wife's bedroom. She's downstairs with her brother, but he'll leave to catch his train in a minute or two, and she'll come up to bed.'

Linster looked at his watch but said nothing.

'Please understand,' Elliston went on, 'that you will get no money if you don't succeed . . .'

'In killing the lady,' Linster finished for him, with a smile. 'Yes, I understand, Mr Elliston. It's cash on delivery.' He stepped forward – carefully, because this was the first part of his plan. He was not like some other men he knew. He was not interested in murder if robbery could do the same job . . .

'You have the cash ready, I hope.'

Elliston took a gun from his pocket. 'Don't try that,' he said. 'The money is safe in my bedroom. If you want it, you'll have to finish the job.'

'Of course,' said Linster, smiling.

'You must use both hands,' said Elliston.

Linster looked at the empty arm of the other man's coat. 'Yes, that's sensible,' he said. 'They always look for clues like that.'

'And you must pretend there was a burglary,' said Elliston. 'Take that jewel-box. There's nothing valuable in it, but you could not know that because it's locked.' Still holding his gun, Elliston moved towards the door. 'I'm going to my bedroom where I shall turn my radio on loud.' He opened the door a little. 'That's my wife's brother leaving now. She's tired, and will come up almost at once. I'll return with the money in . . . twenty minutes.'

Elliston left, and soon the sound of music came from another room. Linster looked around for a good place to

'*The money is safe in my bedroom.*'

hide and saw a clothes cupboard. He would not be able to see anything from inside it, but he could still *hear*. He turned off the light and disappeared into the cupboard like a shadow.

Josephine Demessieux, the young and pretty French servant, came into the bedroom and closed the door. In a bored and careless way, she got the bed ready for Mrs Elliston. There was plenty of time because Mrs Elliston was walking to the railway station with her brother. It was something which she had decided to do at the last moment.

Josephine looked around at the beautiful things which Mrs Elliston owned. She put on one of the rings, then a pretty brooch. Next, she put on a short fur coat which made her look very different when she saw herself in the mirror. 'I'm like a real lady,' she thought.

It was then that Linster moved out of the clothes cupboard. He went silently up behind her. He watched her face in the mirror and was still a metre or two away when she saw him and turned. But his left hand was large and fast. It closed around her narrow throat. She made no sound as she died . . .

Linster gently put her body on the bed, then covered her with a blanket. It took only a few minutes to open cupboards and make them look untidy. He looked at the little jewel-box, then threw it under the bed.

When Elliston entered the room again, still with the gun in his hand, he looked at the shape under the blanket. He said, 'It – it's done?'

'Yes,' said Linster. 'It's done.'

'You're sure she's . . . ?'

'Yes, Mr Elliston, she's dead.' Linster pulled a white hand from under the blanket. 'If you don't believe me, feel this.'

But Elliston jumped back, shaking. 'That ring,' he said slowly. 'It's one she almost never—'

'If you don't believe me, feel this.'

Linster dropped the hand. 'The money, Mr Elliston. Five thousand.'

The money was silently put into his hands.

'I'm going now, Mr Elliston,' said Linster. And then, with a smile, said, 'Sorry I can't stay and talk to that pretty little servant that your wife has.'

Elliston looked surprised. 'The – the girl?'

'The girl,' said Linster. 'I looked through the window of your servants' room before I climbed up here, and there she was. Dark. A soft-looking mouth. A pretty girl. I'd recognize *her* again, anywhere. But I had this job to do. And you don't get paid until you've done the job, do you? It's cash on delivery. And a man must live.'

'I don't understand what you're talking about,' said Elliston.

But Linster was already climbing out of the window. 'You will, Mr Elliston,' he said. 'You will.'

GLOSSARY

alarm bell a bell to warn somebody of danger

alibi something to show you were not there when a crime
  happened

blackmail getting money from somebody by saying you will tell
  bad things about them

brooch a pretty pin or piece of jewellery to wear on clothes

burglary breaking into a house to steal

cash money in coins or notes

cloakroom a place to leave coats, hats, etc.

clue something that helps to find the answer to a mystery or
  crime

cottage a small house

deaf not able to hear

delivery the arrival of something that you are waiting for

divorce to finish a marriage by law

dressing-gown a piece of clothing like a coat to wear over
  night-clothes

dumb not able to speak

freight things (to sell or buy) that are taken by train or ship

fur coat a coat made from the soft, thick hair or skin of an
  animal

hammer a tool with a wooden handle and a heavy metal head

handle the part of something (e.g. a knife) which you hold

jewels/jewellery rings, etc. with valuable stones in them

joke something said or done to make people laugh

lover a person you have sex with, but who is not your husband
  or wife

melt to make soft by using heat or fire

myrtle tree   a kind of tree with white flowers

nut   the hard fruit of a tree or bush

overcoat   a long thick coat to wear in cold weather

parcel   something with paper round it, carried or sent by post

priest   a man who looks after a church and its people

railway crossing   a place where a road and a railway line cross each other

rope   very thick strong string

salt-cellar   a small container for salt

servant   somebody who works in another person's house

shilling   an old English coin (there were 20 shillings in a pound)

simple   not very clever

sleeping powder   something taken to help you sleep

soup   a liquid food, made by cooking meat, vegetables, etc. in water

stain   a dirty place on something

throat   the front part of the neck

tie   to put a piece of rope around something or someone

torch   a small electric light which is carried in the hand

whisky   a strong drink

whisper   to speak very quietly

As the Inspector Said
and Other Stories

ACTIVITIES

Before Reading

1 **Read the introduction on the first page of the book, and the back cover. Then answer these questions.**

1 What are Sonia and her handsome lover planning to do?

2 Who is whispering secrets on a train?

3 What can the thirteen-year-old girl do?

4 Why does Dunstan Thwaite decide he must do something?

5 Why does Flambeau think it will be easy to steal the Blue Cross from Father Brown?

6 What does Mr Elliston think is the safest way to do a murder?

2 **The 'golden age' of crime writing – what do you think this means? Choose the best answer (or answers).**

1 Crime stories were very popular in those years.

2 People made a lot of money writing crime stories at that time.

3 There were more people writing crime stories at that time than at any time since then.

4 Crime stories written at that time were exciting and interesting.

5 A lot of famous writers wrote crime stories then.

3 Look at the five story titles, and then try to guess which of the five sentences below belongs to each title.

As the Inspector Said . . .
The Man Who Cut Off My Hair
The Railway Crossing
The Blue Cross
Cash on Delivery

1 Somebody is killed by a train.
2 A priest tells other passengers on a train that he's carrying something valuable.
3 A detective inspector gives somebody an idea for a murder plan.
4 One man tells another, 'Please understand that you will get no money if you don't succeed . . .'
5 A girl loses something and gets angry.

4 In the first story, *As the Inspector Said . . .*, what do you think is going to happen? Choose Y (yes), N (no), or P (perhaps) for each sentence.

1 Sonia kills her husband. Y/N/P
2 Sonia's lover kills her husband. Y/N/P
3 Sonia steals her husband's old silver. Y/N/P
4 Sonia's husband kills Sonia. Y/N/P
5 Sonia's husband kills her lover. Y/N/P
6 Sonia kills her lover. Y/N/P

While Reading

Read *As the Inspector Said . . .*, then answer these questions.

1 What did the inspector suggest to Robert, and why?
2 When did Sonia shake Robert to wake him up?
3 What did Sonia think when she heard the shot?
4 Why was Sonia waiting before she called the police?
5 Why did Robert clean his gun before he put it in his desk?

Read *The Man Who Cut Off My Hair*. Choose the best question-word for these questions, and then answer them.

Who / Why / Where / What

1 . . . was 'worth at least a hundred' in Myrtle Cottage?
2 . . . was Judith so angry with the man with blue eyes?
3 . . . did Judith promise herself she would not forget?
4 . . . had the thieves left a parcel of jewels?
5 . . . were the police able to catch the thieves?
6 . . . wished he had cut Judith's throat?

Read *The Railway Crossing*. Thwaite has made a check-list for his murder plan and his alibi. Put the list in the right order, and then say what went wrong with his plan.

1 Put body on railway line for freight train to run over.
2 Shout 'Goodnight' and close front door loudly.
3 Move hands of watch and clock forward by ten minutes.

4 Walk home, go into the house through the study door.

5 Walk to the railway station with Dunn.

6 Put sleeping powder in whisky bottle.

7 Call Jane, ask for coffee, make sure she sees clock.

8 Put hands of clock and watch to the right time.

9 Hit Dunn on head with hammer.

10 Put hammer and torch in my coat pockets.

Read *The Blue Cross*. Who said this, and to whom? Who or what were they talking about?

1 'Do you play this joke on your customers every morning?'

2 'Did they knock over your apples?'

3 'I was sure that I'd put four shillings on that bill.'

4 'That will pay for the window.'

5 'It's easily done, Father Brown, easily done!'

6 'She has posted it to a friend of mine in Westminster.'

7 'Do not take off your hat to me, my friend.'

Before you read the last story, *Cash on Delivery*, can you answer these questions?

1 What does 'cash on delivery' usually mean?

2 What do you think will be 'delivered' in this story?

3 Why must somebody pay for this delivery in cash?

Now read the story, and then answer this question.

4 *'You will, Mr Elliston,' said Linster. 'You will.'*
   What is Linster talking about?

After Reading

1 **Perhaps this is what some of the characters in the stories were thinking. Which five characters were they (one from each story), and what was happening in the story at that moment?**

1 How dark it is under these trees! It seems an awfully long way, and I don't feel very well. I just can't keep my eyes open. I think I'll sit down for a minute and have a little rest . . .

2 Twenty minutes to wait, and then I shall be free. I hope he's good at his job – I don't want to hear any screams. Perhaps I'll turn the radio up a bit louder.

3 I don't know what's been happening here. This poor, poor child! I must call the doctor at once. I can see that all my silver has gone, but I'll worry about that later.

4 I know those two are planning something. Perhaps this is the chance that I've been waiting for. Yes, here it is, in my pocket. Now, very quietly to the top of the stairs, then turn on the light – Aaargh!

5 The best moment will be when we're getting off the bus because he'll be in a hurry to pick up all his parcels. I'll offer to help him, and can easily make the change then.

2 **Sonia and Charles (in *As the Inspector Said . . .*) are planning Robert's murder. Complete their conversation. (Use as many words as you like.)**

SONIA: Let's go over the plan again. That night, Robert and I will go to bed at the usual time. At two o'clock you'll

_____.

CHARLES: Right. And when you hear me, you'll wake Robert and _____.

SONIA: But what do I do if he telephones the police from the bedroom and _____.

CHARLES: You must _____.

SONIA: I'll try. All right. He goes downstairs. I wait until I hear _____.

CHARLES: But wait a bit first. You must give me _____.

SONIA: Yes, of course! How long _____?

CHARLES: To be safe, about _____.

SONIA: I'm afraid. What if something _____?

CHARLES: Don't worry, nothing _____ .

3 **But the plan did go wrong. Can you think of answers to these questions, to explain what really happened?**

1 Sonia heard a door banged open, and then the sound of running feet outside the house. Was this
   a) Charles?
   b) Robert?
   c) a third person, and if so, who was it?

2 And what happened to Robert's silver?

4 **Judith is writing to a friend about the man who cut off her hair. Join the parts of sentences to make a short paragraph.**

1 You won't know me next time we meet . . .

2 When I was passing Mr Colegate's cottage last week . . .

3 They caught me and tied me to a chair, . . .

4 He thought that would frighten me, . . .

5 After that, I watched their lips very carefully, . . .

6 The police caught the thieves in a shop in London . . .

7 but it didn't – it just made me very, very angry!

8 I saw two men inside, stealing his silver.

9 because my hair is now very short!

10 and now the man who cut off my hair is in prison!

11 so I found out where they were going next.

12 and then one of them got a knife and cut off all my hair.

5 **Complete this newspaper story about the 'railway crossing' murder with the linking words below. (Use each one once.)**

although / and / and / because / because / before / but / if / in order to / so / so / what / when / which / who

Did Dunstan Thwaite really murder John Dunn? _____ he told the police that he planned to kill Dunn, he said that he did not actually do it. This was Thwaite's story. He invited Dunn, _____ was blackmailing him, to his home, _____ gave him some whisky with a sleeping powder in it. He changed the time on his clock and his watch, _____ give himself an alibi, _____ his murder plan went wrong. He forgot to take his keys with him _____ he walked with Dunn to the railway crossing, _____ he went home, leaving Dunn to walk to the station alone. Dunn probably stopped to rest on the crossing _____ he was feeling sleepy, _____ was killed by the train _____ went through at 10.30. _____ Thwaite's story was true, was that murder or an accidental death?

The police did not believe Thwaite, _____ Dunn was killed at 10.30, and this was seven minutes _____ the servant opened the front door to let Thwaite back in. Now both men are dead, _____ we will never know _____ really happened.

6 **What do *you* think about this murder story? Do you agree (A) or disagree (D) with these ideas?**

1 Thwaite was a murderer. He left Dunn near the railway crossing when he knew that he was feeling ill and sleepy.

2 Thwaite planned to murder Dunn, so it was right for him to get the death punishment.

7 **Valentin (in *The Blue Cross*) wrote a report about the clever clues that Father Brown left for him to follow. Use the notes from Valentin's notebook to write the report.**

- restaurant / London / salt / sugar / wet stains on wall
- fruit shop / apples knocked over / cards / nuts / oranges
- restaurant / Hampstead / broken window / bill / four / fourteen shillings
- sweet-shop / Bullock Street / sweets / parcel / address in Westminster

8 **What do the police say to Mr Elliston, after Josephine's death? Put their conversation in the right order, and write in the speakers' names. Mr Elliston speaks first (number 4).**

1 _____ 'What burglar, Mr Elliston?'

2 _____ 'That's not possible!'

3 _____ 'There was no burglar, sir. Now, we would like you to come down to the police station with us.'

4 _____ 'I didn't hear the burglar at all. I had the radio on.'

5 _____ 'Under the bed? Are – are you sure?'

6 _____ 'But the burglar killed her!'

7 _____ 'Yes. Here it is. And the marks on the girl's throat show that she was killed with one hand. A left hand.'

8 _____ 'The burglar who stole my wife's jewels and—'

9 _____ 'Oh yes, it is. A strong man, like yourself, could easily kill a girl with one hand.'

10 _____ 'But we found your wife's jewel-box under the bed.'

9 **Here are some different titles for the five stories. Which titles go best with each story?**

Mr Colegate's Silver   Death of a Blackmailer

The Body on the Bed   The Parcel and the Priest

A Careful Man   Watch Their Lips

Strange Clues   Nothing Will Go Wrong

The Left-Handed Murder   The Ten-Minute Alibi

10 **Which story did you like best, and which did you like least? Explain why.**

ABOUT THE AUTHORS

G. K. CHESTERTON

Gilbert Keith Chesterton (1874–1936) began writing for newspapers and magazines, but he went on to write poetry, novels, and many volumes of essays. But he is best remembered today for his detective stories about Father Brown, a Roman Catholic priest who understands the criminal mind and who can find the answers to all kinds of mysteries. Father Brown first appeared in *The Innocence of Father Brown* (1911).

EDMUND CRISPIN

Edmund Crispin (1921–1978), whose real name was Bruce Montgomery, began his working life as a teacher but soon became a full-time writer and musician. He wrote music for films, television, and radio, and also wrote for many newspapers and magazines. He wrote only eight detective novels – the most famous is probably *The Moving Toyshop* – but more than fifty short stories.

FREEMAN WILLS CROFTS

Freeman Wills Crofts (1879–1957) was a railway engineer who used what he knew about trains and railways in many of his books and stories. He was very good at mysteries involving timetables and alibis. One of his best-known murder mysteries is *The Cask*, and his most famous detective was Inspector French.

CYRIL HARE

Cyril Hare (1900–1958), whose real name was Alfred Alexander Gordon Clark, worked in the law, first as a lawyer and finally as a judge. He wrote ten crime novels and many very clever short stories.

RICHARD MARSH

Richard Marsh (1857–1915) began writing for boys' magazines when he was only twelve years old. He wrote more than seventy novels, although not all of them were about crime. His most famous book was *The Beetle*, which first appeared in a weekly magazine called *Answers*.

JOHN ESCOTT, who has retold these stories for the Oxford Bookworms Library, himself writes crime and mystery stories. He lives and works in Bournemouth, on the south coast of England.

OXFORD BOOKWORMS LIBRARY

Classics • *Crime & Mystery* • *Factfiles* • *Fantasy & Horror*
Human Interest • *Playscripts* • *Thriller & Adventure*
True Stories • *World Stories*

The OXFORD BOOKWORMS LIBRARY provides enjoyable reading in English, with a wide range of classic and modern fiction, non-fiction, and plays. It includes original and adapted texts in seven carefully graded language stages, which take learners from beginner to advanced level. An overview is given on the next pages.

All Stage 1 titles are available as audio recordings, as well as over eighty other titles from Starter to Stage 6. All Starters and many titles at Stages 1 to 4 are specially recommended for younger learners. Every Bookworm is illustrated, and Starters and Factfiles have full-colour illustrations.

The OXFORD BOOKWORMS LIBRARY also offers extensive support. Each book contains an introduction to the story, notes about the author, a glossary, and activities. Additional resources include tests and worksheets, and answers for these and for the activities in the books. There is advice on running a class library, using audio recordings, and the many ways of using Oxford Bookworms in reading programmes. Resource materials are available on the website <www.oup.com/bookworms>.

The *Oxford Bookworms Collection* is a series for advanced learners. It consists of volumes of short stories by well-known authors, both classic and modern. Texts are not abridged or adapted in any way, but carefully selected to be accessible to the advanced student.

You can find details and a full list of titles in the *Oxford Bookworms Library Catalogue* and *Oxford English Language Teaching Catalogues*, and on the website <www.oup.com/bookworms>.

THE OXFORD BOOKWORMS LIBRARY
GRADING AND SAMPLE EXTRACTS

STARTER • 250 HEADWORDS

present simple – present continuous – imperative –
can/cannot, must – *going to* (future) – simple gerunds …

Her phone is ringing – but where is it?

Sally gets out of bed and looks in her bag. No phone. She looks under the bed. No phone. Then she looks behind the door. There is her phone. Sally picks up her phone and answers it. *Sally's Phone*

STAGE 1 • 400 HEADWORDS

… past simple – coordination with *and*, *but*, *or* –
subordination with *before*, *after*, *when*, *because*, *so* …

I knew him in Persia. He was a famous builder and I worked with him there. For a time I was his friend, but not for long. When he came to Paris, I came after him – I wanted to watch him. He was a very clever, very dangerous man. *The Phantom of the Opera*

STAGE 2 • 700 HEADWORDS

… present perfect – *will* (future) – *(don't) have to, must not, could* –
comparison of adjectives – simple *if* clauses – past continuous –
tag questions – *ask/tell* + infinitive …

While I was writing these words in my diary, I decided what to do. I must try to escape. I shall try to get down the wall outside. The window is high above the ground, but I have to try. I shall take some of the gold with me – if I escape, perhaps it will be helpful later. *Dracula*